TOM PALMER

TAKE TO THE SKIES

WINGS: FLYBOY

WITH ILLUSTRATIONS BY
DAVID SHEPHARD

Barrington Stoke

First published in 2016 in Great Britain by
Barrington Stoke Ltd
18 Walker Street, Edinburgh, EH3 7LP

www.barringtonstoke.co.uk

Text © 2016 Tom Palmer
Illustrations © 2016 David Shephard

A CIP catalogue record for this book is available
from the British Library upon request

ISBN: 978-1-78112-535-9

Printed in China by Leo

"*Flyboy* is a wonderful, warm tale. *Stories highlighting the diversity of Britain's troops during both world wars are rare and this one deserves a wide audience. It is a cracking read.*" **Bali Rai**

For the Gleddings School, Halifax,
to say thank you

Surely one is not fit to live
if one is not ready to face death and smile.

Hardit Singh Malik

ONE

Jatinder took the ball on his chest, then let it drop to his feet. Perfect control. He looked up to see that he had three options.

One, shoot from 40 metres.

Two, knock the ball back to Greg, the keeper, who was standing on the edge of his area.

Three, thread a pass through to Rachel on the wing.

Jatinder made up his mind and stroked the ball wide, taking three defenders out of the game with a neat slide rule pass.

Rachel controlled it, ready to fire a cross into the penalty area.

And now Jatinder was running. Running hard with a tall blond defender following like his shadow. Jatinder was determined to be on the end of the cross. That's what he was all about. Mastering midfield, then breaking into the box.

As he ran, Jatinder ignored the sky-bursting noise of the fighter plane that was coming in to land at the RAF airbase near by. He angled his run towards the penalty area. He ran as fast as he could, but not quite fast enough to outrun the defender powering along beside him.

Jatinder watched Rachel fire a cross in from the right. He heard the thwack of her boot on the ball and he sped up again, then got ready to break into the area, just as the defender nudged him with his shoulder.

Jatinder went down and hit the ground hard. Tumbled. Cried out.

The ref's whistle blew.

Free kick to Jatinder's team, right on the edge of the area.

"Are you OK? Do you want to take it?" Rachel jogged over to Jatinder, gasping for breath. "You earned it."

Jatinder nodded and let Rachel help him stand. His ankle was sharp with pain, but he wanted this. It was well within his range. He had practised this kind of free kick at home on his own, hammering the garage door time after time in the top or bottom corners when everyone else was out.

Rachel handed Jatinder the ball.

He turned it in his hands and squinted at the goal so he could check out the position of the keeper. A little too far off his line. Jatinder could get the ball up and over the wall and the keeper, drop it into the net.

He placed the ball.

The ref's whistle went again.

Jatinder stepped backwards.

Most of the players were bunched around the defending team's wall, ready to defend or attack after the free kick. Only Rachel was to Jatinder's right, with two defenders marking her loosely.

Jatinder stepped back three paces, breathed in, then out. The keeper was even further off his line now, calling to his wall. Bad tactics on his part.

Jatinder could do this. He knew he could.

He moved towards the ball, and his eye caught the top left corner of the goal, the corner he was going to target.

Then, with everything lined up, Jatinder played the free kick short. To his right. To Rachel.

He felt a hot surge of anger rush over him. Why had he done that? Why hadn't he had the go at goal that he'd set up so carefully?

What was that all about?

TWO

Jatinder was still burning up with fury at himself as he walked home ahead of Rachel and Greg.

They were on their way back to the house where they were staying for the week. Most of the children at the Football Summer School were sleeping in dorms next to the school. But Jatinder, Greg and Rachel had got last-minute places and so they were staying with a couple called Steve and Esther in their house on the old abandoned airfield that lay between the school and the new RAF airbase.

Steve and Esther's place was called Trenchard House. As soon as Jatinder's mum dropped him off there, Jatinder was fascinated by the house and its grounds. He'd dumped his bag in his room and set off to explore. In the woods that surrounded the house he found old buildings connected to the First and Second World War airbase, including a hangar that was overgrown with grass. Jatinder also found traces of the old runway crumbling under the roots of trees that had pushed their way up past its surface. Trenchard House itself was where the pilots used to stay. It was a big maze of a place with rambling rooms and staircases, and it was decorated with photos of long-ago pilots in brown uniforms, in old brown picture frames.

Jatinder felt that the house and its grounds had a strange vibe, too – there was something almost magical about the place. It had a feel that made it more than just a wood, some old ruined buildings and a house. It was like another world.

But today Jatinder didn't care about the old airbase as he stomped home ahead of the others. Ahead of them, because he didn't want to walk with them. He was still spitting about the free kick he'd taken. Or not taken. It was really bugging him.

His head buzzed with questions. Why hadn't he had a shot at goal? Why had he played a short pass to Rachel?

Jatinder knew he might have hit the target if he'd gone for it. It was a risk – he'd have looked stupid if he'd fluffed it. A risk, followed by a great goal – if only he'd taken that risk.

And, really, he knew the answers to the questions in his head. It was no mystery. This was always his problem. When it came to the big moments in a game – in his life – Jatinder always played it safe. He never took a risk.

That was it.

If he never took a risk, he'd never look stupid in front of others.

But if he never took a risk, he'd never do anything that stood out – or learn to get better.

Jatinder had been striding along, lost in the circles of his own thoughts, and now he was well ahead of the others. He was in the thick of the woods, where shafts of sunlight coming down through the branches made the trees seem even denser and darker.

And that was when he saw him for the first time. There was a man standing ahead of him on the path. There was nothing strange in that. This was a public footpath and people were up and down it all the time, walking dogs, running, out for a stroll. But there *was* something strange about this man – it was the clothes he was wearing. A long dark coat. Heavy boots. A hat that could have been a turban – he was too far away to tell for sure, but Jatinder felt certain it was a turban.

The man looked lost. Or perhaps he had lost something. The air seemed to whistle around him. Jatinder shivered.

All of a sudden the woods felt very cold.

Jatinder took a few more steps and then stopped. The man had disappeared. It was hard to tell where he had gone.

THREE

Jatinder sat outside Trenchard House and stared into the woods. He was looking for the man he'd seen there, as well as going over and over the free kick in his mind.

Now there were two things worrying him. Two things he couldn't make sense of.

"Get a grip," he told himself as he gazed past the trees at the huge shape of the old aircraft hangar under its overgrown roof of grass and shrubs, with its sad, smashed windows and rusting metal doors.

Jatinder wished he could just give up this week at the summer school and go home. But if he went home he'd have to tell his mum and dad why he'd given up.

What would he say to them? That he missed the chance to take a good free kick? That would sound stupid. Really stupid. A tiny, nothing sort of thing to explain why he was so fed up.

But it wasn't just a tiny thing in his head. It was a big thing. So big that he just couldn't shake it. It stayed in his mind and grew there. The more he told himself that it was nothing, the bigger it became.

It became a stupid big thing.

Since the game, Jatinder had been stepping up to the ball in his mind over and over, and each time he tried to take the free kick properly. But he never did. He always played it wide to Rachel.

Stupid. Stupid. Stupid.

"It doesn't matter," he told himself out loud. "Just do it right next time."

"Jatinder?"

Jatinder turned round to see Esther, the woman who was looking after him that week, standing just inside the house. Jatinder liked her – she was a nice woman, always calm and always smiling, with short dark hair that framed her face. She didn't mention that she'd caught Jatinder talking to himself.

"What's up?" Esther asked.

"Nothing." Jatinder shrugged. "Not really."

"Not really ... but a bit?" Esther smiled.

"Nothing big."

"So, something small, then?" Esther smiled again. "They can be the worst, eh?"

"I suppose," Jatinder agreed. He couldn't decide if Esther would get what was bothering him.

"Tell me about it," she said, and she sat down next to him so they were both looking out into the trees.

"It's stupid," he mumbled.

"Maybe so, but tell me anyway."

So Jatinder fixed his eyes on the airfield and the woods and told Esther about the free kick.

Esther listened, and nodded when it was a good time to nod. And – for a while – it felt good to tell someone else about his problems. But, as Jatinder listened to himself, he wondered if what he was talking about was important at all. Wasn't he just whining, looking for problems where there were none? All of a sudden, he'd had enough.

"Can we talk about something else?" he asked Esther.

Esther turned to him, her eyebrows raised in surprise.

"Please?"

"OK. You're the boss." She smiled at him, but she still looked a bit worried. "What about?"

"This place," Jatinder said. "So ... it was an airfield?"

"Yes, in the two world wars," Esther told him. "The RAF were based here."

"The RAF? Like Spitfires?"

She nodded. "Yes. All that. It's hard to believe now, isn't it?"

"Kind of," Jatinder said. "But the pilots on the walls and in all those books – were they from here?"

"Some of them." Esther paused. "In fact ..."

"What?"

"STEVE?" Esther shouted into the house, then she turned to Jatinder again. "There was one very famous pilot who flew from here ... He was a Sikh, like you, but that's not why I think you might find him interesting."

As Esther spoke, Steve appeared at the door with a tea towel in his hands. He was about as old as Jatinder's grandad, but still tall, lean and handsome with close-cropped, grey-peppered hair.

"Hello, Jatinder," he said. "Good day?"

Jatinder shrugged.

"That book you read, love," Esther said. "Years ago. About the RFC pilot from India. Where is it?"

"On the shelves." Steve laughed. The bookshelves in Trenchard House were piled high with a jumble of books. "Somewhere."

Esther shook her head. "OK ... can you get it for us, please?"

Steve nodded and disappeared back into the house.

"What's the RFC?" Jatinder asked.

"Royal Flying Corps," Esther explained. "That's what they were called before they became the RAF. They trained and lived here at this airfield."

"We learned about the RAF at school," Jatinder said. "I did a project on Spitfires. I got a really good mark."

Just then Steve came back out from the house and handed a book to Esther. Jatinder caught sight of the cover. A black and white photo of a young man in a turban.

"This the one?" Steve asked.

Esther nodded and Steve passed the book to Jatinder. "Do you like reading then?" he asked.

"Sometimes," Jatinder said. "Depends what the book's about."

"I think you'll like this," Steve said. "Give it a try. That guy on the cover was the first ever Sikh fighter pilot. Hardit Singh Malik."

FOUR

That night Jatinder left Greg playing a game on his phone and Rachel watching TV with Esther.

He'd decided on an early night so he could read the book Steve had given him.

It was one of those old-fashioned books with very long chapters and very small letters that were a bit too close together. But it had some good photos. Jatinder flicked through it, looking at the photos and at the bits that interested him.

He read about Hardit Singh Malik when he was a boy in India. How he'd left home, aged 14, to go to school in Britain. And how – when the

First World War broke out – he'd written to his family to say he wanted to fight.

There was a copy of the letter in the book. One line in it grabbed Jatinder's attention.

Surely one is not fit to live if one is not ready to face death and smile.

Jatinder didn't quite understand what that meant. And he was sleepy now, his eyes wanting to close. He could hear that the wind had picked up outside and he could sense something odd, like the smell in a petrol station.

Jatinder put the book down and was drifting off to sleep when his eyes snapped open.

There was the ghost of a First World War airman in his room. The man from the woods. He wasn't wearing his long leather coat now, but a khaki jacket with a pair of wings on a cloth badge. The RFC wings, Jatinder was sure

of it. The same wings as some of the men in the photos on the walls. He stood in the far corner and cast his eyes around as if he was still lost, until his eyes fell on Jatinder.

Jatinder gasped and grabbed at the side of the bed. He could feel his whole body shaking. He screwed his eyes shut.

It couldn't be true.

Jatinder opened his eyes to prove to himself that there was no one there, that he was just imagining things. But the man was still there.

Jatinder screwed his eyes shut again. He didn't need this. He didn't want it. Not now. Not ever.

"Go away," he whispered. "Please."

When at last he opened his eyes again, the room was empty. The man was gone.

FIVE

Day two at the football summer school and Jatinder gave it his all. Every tackle. Every pass. Every run on and off the ball. His ankle was sore and he was feeling far from 100% confident, but he pushed past it.

He couldn't stop thinking about the visit from the pilot's ghost the night before. It must have been a dream. And what did that line from the Hardit Singh Malik book really mean? It rang true with Jatinder somehow, but he couldn't quite grasp it. Maybe it meant you have to get stuck in or there's no point doing anything. Something like that. So that was what Jatinder was trying to do. He held the words from Hardit Singh Malik in his mind, and he felt his confidence coming back.

'I just need a free kick now,' he said to himself. 'And I'll do it properly this time.'

"You were good today," Greg said as the three of them walked back to Trenchard House. "Loads stronger and much better pace."

"Do you think so? Thanks," Jatinder said. "I just wish ..." He was going to say how he'd wanted a free kick to prove to himself that he could have taken one, but he stopped himself. It was better to return the praise than go on about himself.

"You were pretty sharp too, Greg," he said. "Those saves you made. Amazing."

It worked.

Greg grinned and goofed about, pretending to dive for a ball as they walked into the woods.

That was when Jatinder noticed the light change. It grew cooler in the shade and he looked ahead to see if the ghostly airman was there today. He wasn't.

Jatinder, Rachel and Greg walked past the old buildings, locked up since they were last used over 70 years ago. A plane passed overhead and Jatinder looked up. But not because it was a noisy modern jet like the day before. That one had been gunmetal grey, shaped like a triangle, and flying almost too fast to see. Today's plane was old. Very old. It was a bi-plane, a relic from an air show. It flew on with almost no sound at all and disappeared behind the woods.

Away from the trees, sparkles of sunlight reflected off the windows of Trenchard House. Then, just as they approached the house, a grey cloud passed over the sun. Jatinder's eyes were drawn to his bedroom window.

Without the glare of sun, he thought he could see someone moving about in his room. Maybe Steve hoovering? Or Esther putting some clean kit on his bed?

No.

It wasn't Steve.

It wasn't Esther.

Jatinder could see exactly who it was. It was the man in the uniform. The Sikh pilot.

Jatinder began to sprint across the old airstrip, ignoring the way its uneven concrete and hummocks of grass strained his sore ankle as he ran. He ran away from the calls of Greg and Rachel. Past Esther in the garden. Past Steve in the kitchen. Into the cool of the house, with its old-fashioned rooms. He hit the wooden stairs hard, watched by the photos of old airmen staring out at him with grim looks on their faces.

He had to know. Was he seeing things? He had convinced himself that last night had been a dream. Could it have been some odd reflection of himself in the window? It had to be. Or was there really a ghost? Did ghosts even exist? And, if they did, why had one shown itself to him?

Jatinder felt driven by an urge to see the ghost this time, to talk to him, to tell him to stay, not to go away.

He was gasping for air by the time he reached the top of the stairs. He slowed to a walk, breathed hard and deep as he stepped towards his bedroom door. Then – without stopping, without allowing himself time to be afraid – he pushed the door open.

SIX

Jatinder stood at the door and looked into his bedroom. There was the bed, the far wall, the wardrobe, the window.

But there was no one there. No ghost. No pilot.

"What's up?"

The question made Jatinder jump. He took a sudden, sharp breath and held onto the frame of the door. Steve was standing at the end of the hall behind him.

"I thought ..." Jatinder stopped himself. What had he thought?

Steve said nothing.

"You'll laugh," Jatinder said, to fill the silence. "I thought I saw a man in my room. A pilot."

But Steve didn't laugh. His face was steady and serious, as if he was waiting for Jatinder to say more.

"But it was just a reflection on the window," Jatinder said.

Steve nodded and they looked at each other for a moment. Then Steve changed the subject. "How was it today?" he asked. "The football?"

"OK," Jatinder said. "Not bad."

"Good."

"But I was thinking too much," Jatinder confessed.

"About free kicks?" Steve grinned. "Esther told me. Forget about it."

"No. Not the free kicks. Not just the free kicks. About last night." Jatinder hesitated. "I thought I saw a pilot then, too. In my room. When I was reading your book."

"Ahh ..." Steve said. "Do you know what this house was used for?"

"Steve!" Esther called from the bottom of the stairs. "*Steve*!"

"Hang on, love," Steve called down, then turned back to Jatinder. "What do you think?"

"I know," Jatinder replied. "Pilots lived here."

"That's right," Steve said. "Out there, the bit you walk across with Rachel and Greg, that used to be the airfield. It's so overgrown now you'd hardly know it was an airfield. They didn't have a runway when it started. Just an ordinary, fairly flat field. The pilots would train here first – and then later they'd fly from here on their raids."

"Then they came back and slept in this house?"

"Yes, Jatinder. Except sometimes – after the raids – they didn't come back. You know?"

Jatinder knew and it made him shiver. Had the temperature in the house dropped all of a sudden? It was amazing to think what had happened here, but all he could think to say was, "Oh. OK."

Steve fixed him with his eyes. "Even if you think you are seeing pilots round here every now and then, it doesn't mean anything," he said. "There's a lot of history here. That's all. It's seeped into the house, the woods, the old airfield. But it's just like reflections in windows – nothing to worry about."

Jatinder nodded. What was that supposed to mean? Was Steve trying to say the house was haunted?

Then Esther was jogging up the stairs. "Steven," she said, "I hope you're not telling Jatinder your stupid ghost stories."

"Just history, Ess," Steve said with a shrug. "History, not ghost stories."

Jatinder could tell this was a conversation they'd had more than once.

"Hmmm," Esther said. "Come on, Jatinder. You can help me pick some veg for dinner. Don't get caught up in his crazy ways. He needs to get out more."

Jatinder went with Esther. His thoughts were all over the place. What had Steve been getting at? And what had Esther meant about stupid stories? He felt spooked, unsettled – like a character in his own ghost story.

SEVEN

Jatinder went to bed early again that night. He wanted to read more of the book about Hardit Singh Malik. But there was something else that made him turn in early too. Something that surprised him. He found he wanted to see the ghost again ... if it was a ghost, of course. Even though he was afraid, even though he had no idea what would happen, he still wanted the ghost to reappear.

So he went to bed, tapped the light on his bedside table and read.

He read more about Malik. How they'd not let him in the Flying Corps because his skin was brown, not white. How he'd kept trying and trying and – with help from one of his teachers – how at last he'd become an RFC pilot.

Jatinder read Malik's tips on how to fly a plane, his thoughts on how it *felt* to fly a plane. The adrenaline rush, the sense of being so high above everything and everyone. It sounded fantastic to Jatinder. He liked how the ex-pilot described it in his book. But he didn't like what had happened to Malik when his plane was hit by 450 bullets, two of which went into his leg. He'd come crashing out of the sky, nearly died and was lucky not to be taken prisoner.

As the evening air cooled, the house began to creak around Jatinder. The roof contracted. The floorboards settled. Jatinder knew what was making the noises, that they were normal in an old house like this, but the creaks and sighs still set the hairs up on the back of his neck. Then that smell again – of fuel, like burning petrol. And other noises too. The throb and clatter of machines, of engines. Was someone mowing the grass out on the football pitches? Surely not at this time of night.

Weird.

There *was* something about this house. Steve was right.

Jatinder went back to the book. He focused hard so he could block out the noises and the stink of fuel. And then he got so caught up that it was like he was there, in Malik's plane by his side. He could almost see the flashing lights from outside, feel a lurch in his stomach as the plane rose and fell, sense the blast of cold air that whipped at him like a window had opened in the wind. He ignored it all. He was lost in the book. Totally focused.

It was amazing. Malik's story made Jatinder feel like he actually was in a plane above the battlefields of the First World War. And he was so taken with Malik's adventures, his descriptions of them, that he wished he could see the ghost of the pilot again. Just for a moment.

Then Jatinder looked up, and he couldn't believe his eyes.

The control panel of a plane was right in front of his face. It was wooden, with three or four dials and a small, see-through screen with a heavy leather trim above it. Then, ahead of that, a large black gun pointed at a spinning propeller, which sent flecks of oil at Jatinder's face and the goggles he was wearing.

It was a scene just like the ones Malik had described in his book.

Jatinder felt his body tilt to the left as he was caught by another blast of cold air. It was pure instinct that made him grab the control stick in front of him and move it to the right.

Control stick? What the hell was going on?
Where was his bedside lamp? His duvet? His
book?

'A dream,' he told himself. 'It has to be
another dream.'

Jatinder looked over the side of the cramped
compartment and more cold air blasted his
face and ears. More flecks of oil splattered on
his goggles.

He was level with the clouds.

And there were fields below.

He could see hundreds of miles of land and
sky. And here he was, up here.

His body convulsed. He was not in
Trenchard House. He was not in bed. He was
in a plane high above the world.

Impossible.

Incredible.

Unbearable.

Jatinder felt his guts tighten. He was going to be sick. His body was struggling to cope, but the weird thing was his mind was OK. He felt like he knew what he was doing, that he knew how to fly the plane. He tugged the control stick to the right again, levelling out the plane so that it was heading straight. It was an instinct he didn't understand, but the fact remained – he was in a plane and he was flying it.

But how?

Next Jatinder heard a sharp crack above the loud droning noise of his engine. He looked over the side and saw puffs of smoke. Then his plane jolted violently and a hole appeared in the canvas of the wing not far from his shoulder. His nostrils filled with the sudden sharp stink of fuel.

Someone was shooting at him. He could see them. Clusters of men hundreds of feet below, guns popping and flashing as they fired at him.

There was no question. He was over enemy territory and he was being shot at. Again, just like Malik had described in his book.

Jatinder pulled the control stick and the nose of the plane lifted. He had to get out of here. He had to go up, get away from the gunfire.

And that's what he managed to do. Soon there was just the noise of the engine. No gunfire.

So now what should he do? Turn the plane round and head back the way he had come? But where was that? He had no idea.

He decided he would turn the plane round, close his eyes and aim straight ahead. That was it. Then this nightmare would end. That must be what this was. A nightmare, triggered by Malik's book.

Jatinder flew on. The skies were empty. There were no other planes. No birds. That's how he knew it was a dream. It just didn't feel real.

And then his engine cut out. The smell of fuel became more intense now. Jatinder knew what had happened. His tank had been hit. The sharp smell had been the fuel draining out of his plane. Now the fuel was gone.

Jatinder listened to the wind rushing past as his plane shuddered and slowed. It was going down, with him in it. And as it sank and his body lurched with it, Jatinder understood that this was no dream.

It was horrid, awful – and real.

EIGHT

Just as Jatinder realised that he knew how to fly, he couldn't do it any more, because he was falling out of the sky, powerless, out of control, facing death. He looked at the plane's wings, stretched out to his right and left. They were so flimsy, wobbling in the wind as the body of the plane juddered and shuddered.

The fact was that his plane had been hit. Nothing else really mattered.

But this whole situation was impossible. It made playing football seem the easiest thing in the world. Where was the risk in taking a free kick? What real danger was there to face there?

"Football?" he almost shouted at himself. His face was freezing in the cold air and his ears were burning at the same time. "This is no time to think about football."

This dream. This story. Whatever it was, it wasn't about football.

Something calm inside Jatinder knew he was going to die.

But, at the same time, he heard a hard voice in his head. "No way!" it said. "Sort yourself out. Get this plane under control before it crashes into the ground."

Jatinder snatched at the control stick, then pulled it towards himself. It didn't shift. He pulled again and again, using strength he didn't know he had. Still nothing. Then he forced his feet down onto a pedal, and somehow he managed to lift the plane's nose. The plane levelled and began to slow again.

How did he do that?

He had no idea. But it seemed he really did know how to fly this thing, even after his fuel tank had been shot to pieces. And he knew that it was a Sopwith Camel. Maybe he'd learned that from Malik's book? Maybe Malik had described a Sopwith Camel and how to keep it aloft?

So *was* he doomed? *Was* there hope?

Jatinder heard that cold voice again. "Keep the plane level, keep it moving. Look for somewhere safe and land it."

'OK,' Jatinder thought. 'I can do that.'

Perhaps he *could* save himself.

He was lower now. The world was closer. Fences and trees. Animals in herds. Small clusters of houses along winding roads.

Jatinder was looking for a large field without fences and walls too close together, where he could touch down, just like the pilots had done on the airfield next to Trenchard House.

That was it. A place to crash land. He might be over enemy territory, but he'd be safer on the ground than up here in his shattered plane.

Jatinder wondered for a nano-second how he knew all this about where he was, about what plane he was flying. But it was only a nano-second. There was no time to think. He had to take action. Take action or die.

Jatinder scanned the countryside below, and saw a stretch of land along a river. It wasn't fenced off. The surface looked even enough to cope with. There was a forest at the far end, but, if he could get down before that, he might be able to land the plane.

Jatinder couldn't think about what would happen after he landed. Just about a smooth landing. Not a rending crash, then dying in a wreck of burning wood and canvas.

First he took the plane into a steeper descent. Then, when he was low enough, he lifted its nose to level it out again.

This was it.

Lower.

Right on the foot rudder. Keep it level.

He could hear the rush of the water in the river as well as the air around him. And it felt warmer down here, out of the clouds.

Lower still.

Now he could see the patterns made by the surface of the fields.

This was it.

Down.

Plenty of space ahead.

Push the stick forward. Slowly. Ever so slowly, so as not to overdo it and pitch the plane nose-down.

And then despair. He could see ridges, shallow furrows in the field. He knew that there was no way he could land the plane across those. He had to land parallel with them or not at all. The plane – this flimsy kite – would be smashed to pieces.

So Jatinder turned the Sopwith Camel to the left. A sudden easy turn so as to be in line with the ridges and land between them, not across them. That was his plan.

But, as he made his move, he could see that it was too late. The field was long, but it wasn't

wide. Jatinder snatched the control stick and pulled at it, giving his plane a lift over a sudden hedgerow.

Then trees. So close. Jatinder needed to be higher, to gain as much lift as he could. His plane clipped the tops of the trees with a ripping sound.

Now another field. Another hedge. And all the time his dying plane was losing height.

The next field had a haystack in the middle. Jatinder knew he would make it over the haystack, but no further, because the fields beyond the haystack were full. Not full of cows or crops or trees. They were full of men. Men in tents and with machinery. Jatinder knew without a shadow of a doubt that it was a German army camp. He recognised their flags. Black, white and red with a bold image of an eagle at the centre. And he knew that his plane was going to crash into the enemy camp.

Jatinder undid the belt that strapped him into the cramped cockpit and gripped the sides of the plane with both hands. He had made a decision.

He would jump.

He would jump and land in the haystack.

It was a crazy idea. If he missed the haystack he would die. But he had no choice. If he didn't jump he would die. And wasn't this only a dream? It couldn't be real. If he died he would wake up safe in his bed like he always did after a bad dream.

Jatinder scrambled out of the cockpit, clinging onto the side of the plane, his feet on the wing. Warm air streamed past him with a force that made him yet more unsteady. And the strange clothes he was wearing didn't help either. They felt rough against his skin and the heavy brown material dragged him down.

As he paused before his jump, Jatinder thought about Malik. What had he said? You had to be ready to face death with a smile.

Did the pilot really believe that? Is that how he felt when he was flying?

"One ... two ... three ..." Jatinder counted himself down to his jump. Then, as the plane tumbled from the sky, he pushed his body out into the unknown.

NINE

Jatinder's chest felt like it was caving in, exploding. Light and colour flashed in his mind.

Air rushed past his ears.

His own shouts echoed around him.

His eyes were screwed tight shut against the terrible fact that he was about to feel the most horrendous pain.

Jatinder was falling.

Then there was the sound of crunching or ripping. But he felt no pain. And he was sneezing. Sneezing over and over again.

Had he hit the haystack?

Was he still alive?

Jatinder opened his eyes and stared up at a huge sky above him, blue with wisps of white drifting across it. OK, so he wasn't back in bed at Trenchard House.

At last Jatinder stopped sneezing and breathed in as deeply as he could. He sucked at the air, feeling like he could take in the whole sky. He had never felt so happy.

He'd dared to jump.

He'd landed safely. It was a miracle.

Now he was laughing. He put aside all his worries about why he was in the haystack, about how he had pitched up here a hundred years back in time – and as a pilot, no less. None of it mattered.

Jatinder had survived. He'd faced death and smiled. He was certainly smiling now. It was just like Malik had said.

But then he heard a crash and a crackling and saw a dark ribbon of cloud drift across the sky. His nostrils filled with the stink of smoke. He rolled onto his side and spotted a tree on fire about 400 yards away. His plane was tangled among its branches and together they were burning. Wood and canvas and metal all in flames.

Jatinder knew that he could have been part of that burning. He could have been turning to ashes in that tree.

He stared in horror at the fire. He wasn't laughing now, especially as he could hear another noise getting louder and louder. There was an engine coming towards him. Jatinder peered over the top of his haystack to see a car stop very close. He was looking straight at two men in uniform.

Germans.

The enemy.

But he was the enemy to them too.

What would they do to him?

Shoot him?

Jatinder knew it was hopeless to try to run. They were in a large open field and the Germans had a car and guns. He would be an easy target.

He rolled onto his back and tried to bring his breathing back under control. He took in his huge black boots and his thick brown trousers. Under his long leather coat he had on a thinner jacket with the letters RFC on a set of wings over his left pocket. Here, in this time, Jatinder was an adult, a pilot – he looked just like one of the men in the old photos on the walls of Trenchard House.

But, man or boy, Jatinder now had to face an armed enemy who had just shot him out of the sky.

TEN

"Halt!"

The noise of the car engine cut out and Jatinder heard a shout and more sharp words in German from below.

Acting on instinct, he put his hands above his head and pieces of straw fell from the chest and arms of his leather coat. Jatinder could feel his heart pounding, a feeling made worse by the heavy, hot clothes he was wearing. All the joy of his safe landing was gone. Instead, a cold feeling was pushing its way along his veins, as if his blood was draining out of him into the hay.

Would he be shot? Up here on this haystack?

Jatinder raised his head slowly. Two men in grey uniforms were pointing their rifles at him. The rifles had long blades attached to their ends – bayonets.

"What do you want me to do?" Jatinder called down to them, and he was startled by his own deep voice.

The men stared at Jatinder, then at each other. It was as if they had no idea who or what he was. They lowered their guns, as if confused by his words.

Jatinder didn't know, but he guessed they'd never seen a Sikh before.

He put his hands up to his turban. It was a proper man's turban, but it had been knocked to one side by the fall from the plane. The

Germans watched him as he put it back on straight.

Next Jatinder touched his face to find that he had a full beard too.

He was wearing a man's clothes, he spoke like a man and had a beard like a man. He was still a Sikh, but he was a Sikh pilot in the heat of a long-ago war. He certainly wasn't Jatinder, a 12-year-old boy on his summer holidays.

His mind was spinning. This was madness. How and when would it end?

The Germans bundled Jatinder into a vehicle that looked more like a horse-drawn carriage with an engine than a car. Its seats were made of stiff black leather. It bounced along the track tossing Jatinder and the two Germans into the air every few seconds. Jatinder sat on the front seat beside one of the soldiers. The second soldier was behind him.

The tip of his bayonet jabbed Jatinder's arm every time the car jolted.

Jatinder stared at the sky. He was a prisoner. There was nowhere he could jump to now. And if he tried to run away he would have no chance. He'd be shot.

They were heading towards the military camp. Stretched out in front of them were hundreds and hundreds of tents, flags, soldiers, trucks and other vehicles. There were even some planes off to the left, hidden among the trees.

Jatinder was thinking about what might come next. He'd seen the news on TV at home. He'd seen how prisoners of war had terrible things done to them. He closed his eyes, worried he might vomit. Should he tell the Germans who he really was? A British boy who had fallen out of the sky and had also fallen one hundred years back in time?

Would they believe him?

Of course not.

Would they shoot him?

Perhaps.

The car passed a checkpoint. Two soldiers stared at Jatinder like they were looking at an animal in a cage. Then their hard, battle-weary faces began to smile. And Jatinder could hear applause.

Jatinder realised that everyone at the camp entrance was looking at him, and even coming up to the car. They were all smiling. And clapping too.

Why?

Who did they think he was?

What now?

The car stopped and Jatinder closed his eyes, just for a few seconds. He wanted to try to keep calm. To be prepared.

Then a voice said, "You are welcome, Officer. Let me help you out of the car. Are you hurt?" They were English words spoken with a curt German accent.

Jatinder opened his eyes to see a soldier standing before him. He was tall and blond, with a clipped moustache. There was a challenge in his dark eyes, but his face had a kindness about it.

"Excuse please our welcome," the soldier said. "We have never witnessed a man cheat death like this. You jump from plane and land in the hay. Amazing." He clapped again and then, as if he had just remembered where he was, he said, "I am Lieutenant Böll. You are our very welcome guest."

Jatinder couldn't believe it. He was being treated like a hero. The enemy saw him as a brave man and respected him for it. Jatinder liked that feeling of respect and admiration but, even so, he had no idea what was going to happen next.

ELEVEN

Lieutenant Böll took Jatinder to be checked over by the camp doctor, and then he made him an offer.

"You would like to see how we are here?" he asked. "To see our aircraft, compare them to yours. I know I would like to take this chance myself."

Jatinder said yes. He was more confused than he'd ever been in his life, but it seemed wise to play along and be a good guest. Or was he fooling himself? Perhaps the best he could do was be a good prisoner?

He followed the German soldier past stables filled with horses and past rows and rows of wooden boxes of bombs. The tour ended in a large area of forest on the edge of the army camp. Among the trees, Jatinder saw the German planes again.

"These are … how do you say in England? … our pride and our joy." Böll smiled.

"Yes – pride and joy," Jatinder said. "Very nice."

"These are our Fokkers," Böll enthused. "Our superb new fighters from Berlin. These planes will win the war for us. We will send them to destroy your Sopwith Camels. Your Royal Flying Corps. They will drive you back into the sea. They are magnificent, yes?"

Jatinder looked at the fighter planes. Each one had a menacing machine gun mounted at the front. He tried to remember what Malik had said in his book. Had the Sopwith Camels defeated the Fokkers? He hoped so.

"I wish you could join us to fly these machines," Böll said. "They can reach speeds of 107 m.p.h. and can carry twice as many bullets as your Sopwith Camels. There is nothing like them in the world. They will win the war for Germany."

The German's boasting was starting to make Jatinder's blood boil. "What about the Spitfire?" he snapped, remembering his school project about the planes of the Second World War.

Böll stopped and glared at him. "What is Spitfire?" he demanded.

"A plane. A Second ..." Jatinder stopped himself. He realised he was talking about a plane that didn't yet exist. If he wasn't careful he would betray his country, give away secrets that needed to be kept for another 30 years and more.

Böll had taken out a notepad and pencil. "Tell me more about this Fire Spitter."

Jatinder sighed. He'd have to tell him something now. And he was rattled enough to want to tell Böll something to shut him up and make him realise that German planes weren't always the best.

"I don't know much," Jatinder said in the end. "It's a monoplane. It flies at 367 m.p.h. and has eight machine guns."

Böll's face was creased with anxiety. And then he tapped his notepad with his pencil. "Ah … you are joking," he said with a thin smile. "The British sense of humour." He winked at Jatinder and started to guffaw.

Jatinder laughed along, glad he could remember his history. The Spitfire had stopped the German invasion of Britain in 1940. It was an odd feeling, but that fact made him feel proud. Just like Malik had made him proud.

Jatinder was living in Malik's world, in his time. That much was clear. It felt like a kind of madness, but it was clear all the same.

And then Jatinder was struck by an even greater moment of clarity. He saw that it was time to stop behaving like Jatinder. Polite. Respectful. Safe. It was time to behave like his hero now. He was a pilot whose job it was to fight to save Britain from the enemy. He had shown himself and others that he could be brave, that he could do something out of the ordinary. Something had changed for Jatinder.

"May I look at one of your Fokkers?" Jatinder asked. "More closely?"

Jatinder noticed that Böll waited a second before smiling.

"Yes. Of course," he said. "Come."

They walked over to the planes.

"Look at it," Böll said, in full flow again. "This engineering is the finest in the world. The German expertise in flight is vastly superior. We understand that the war in the air will dominate the 20th century. Yes?"

Jatinder nodded. The engineering was impressive, but he could see how very fragile these planes were. They were still only canvas stretched over a wooden frame, nothing like the smooth metal shapes of the 21st-century planes he'd seen in the skies over Trenchard House. These Fokkers would be so easy to destroy – a spark or flame and they'd be reduced to ash. Just as he'd seen happen to his own plane.

Jatinder felt a feeling that was new to him. A feeling of anger mixed with a sense of pride in who he was, and a burning desire to do something to stop the enemy. He knew that acting on this feeling would mean taking a risk, a risk like he'd never taken before.

"So," Böll snapped. "You have seen what you wanted to see?"

"Yes," Jatinder said. "I have. Thank you."

He knew there and then that he would take that risk. He would prove himself in this war, just like Malik had done. If he was living in this new world – a world in which he could jump out of a plane and survive – then he could do whatever he wanted. He would take action. And he would take it smiling.

TWELVE

That night Jatinder found himself dining with a group of German pilots. To his surprise, he'd enjoyed the meal, and he had taken the chance to steal a short knife and push it down inside his boot. Just in case.

Now he was being driven away from the German army camp in a rickety car.

"We are to exchange you," Böll informed him above the sound of the engine.

"Exchange me?" Jatinder replied. "I don't understand."

"One of our pilots was captured when he landed his plane behind your lines. Like you.

We are to swap you for him. So now you will be able to fly again."

"Thank you," Jatinder said. He wasn't quite sure if this was the right response.

"I am to be your escort," Böll added. "We are to travel by train."

The car drew up by a stretch of railway track with lines of vehicles and army supplies. The place was thronged with hundreds of men and dozens of horses. Jatinder could smell mud, sweat and horse manure. And burning.

"This train will take us to the front," Böll said. "I will hand you over personally. It will be my honour."

"Thank you," Jatinder said again, but he was distracted by some of the carriages he had seen on the train. They were flatbed carriages – not for people, but for Fokkers. There were at least ten of them on the train.

"More German planes," Böll said proudly, as he followed Jatinder's line of sight. "They are heading to the front – to take on your famous RFC." He pointed at the RFC badge on Jatinder's chest. "Maybe one day we will meet in the skies. That would be an honour for me too."

Jatinder squinted as he studied the German planes. He imagined them in the air, shooting down countless British pilots. For a long time Jatinder said nothing. He was thinking instead about what he could do to stop them.

"I can read your mind, Officer," Böll said.

Jatinder stepped back. Was it so obvious?

"I must warn you," Böll said. "Sabotage is a serious crime. In just one day you will be a free man, back among your own people. If you sabotage those planes, you will be shot on sight. Dead. Please, do not do anything foolish. I would hate to see such a brave man as yourself shot like a dog."

Inside the railway carriage, Böll put a packet of German cigarettes and a box of matches onto the table and smiled.

"Just sit and smoke," he said. "Be calm. You will be with your friends tomorrow."

Jatinder was about to say no, but then he thought again and smiled back at Böll. He might not want the cigarettes, but a box of matches could be very useful indeed. He could start a fire with a box of matches.

But just as he thought that, Jatinder surprised himself by saying, "Rest assured, Böll, I will do nothing foolish."

"Get some rest, my friend," Böll said, and his face was kind again. "Our journey will take time."

Jatinder watched Böll close the door. As it shut, he saw a latch slip down between the door and its frame.

He was locked in – a prisoner.

Jatinder looked out of the window of his compartment. Night was falling. The train had begun to move west, towards the setting sun, where the front line was. Jatinder looked at the sky and wondered if any British pilots were up there now.

As the train pulled out into the countryside, it made its way around a long bend. Jatinder could see the carriages next to his and realised they were the very carriages he'd been looking at earlier, carrying the ten Fokker planes to the front. He would like to stop those planes. He knew that they would be used to kill dozens, maybe hundreds, of British RFC pilots and he wanted to do everything he could to make sure that didn't happen. But as he tried to work out how to do it, the night turned black and all he could see was his reflection in the window of the train.

Jatinder stepped back in shock. For the first time he could see himself as an adult. An RFC uniform, the wings motif on his broad chest. A black turban. A long beard. Jatinder touched his beard and then his turban and it struck him who he looked like. It wasn't a member of his family. It wasn't Hardit Singh Malik. No, he looked like the man who had been haunting him. The ghost from Trenchard House.

'Why me?' he wondered. 'Why am I here? Is there something I am meant to do?'

Jatinder asked his last question aloud and it was as if it answered itself.

He knew now exactly what he had to do.

THIRTEEN

Jatinder used the knife he had stolen at dinner to flip open the lock to his compartment. One easy click and he was no longer a prisoner.

He eased the door open and listened before he stepped out. He had to be sure nobody was there. But it was hard to hear anything above the noise of the train as it clattered along the tracks into the night. Jatinder was going to have to take a risk. He could hear his heart beating as fast as the rattling train. In the past he would have taken this beating to be a sign of fear, a sign that he should stop, do nothing. But today he understood that it was his body giving him courage to face what he had to face, to do what he needed to do.

He peered up and down the corridor. It was dark and gloomy, lit by three flickering lights.

All clear.

Jatinder picked up the box of matches and stepped out into the corridor. He eased his door shut behind him and moved towards the back of the train. He knew that was where the German planes were and, as he reached the end of the carriage, he saw them. A row of ten pristine fighter planes, moonlight shimmering off their wings.

Fokkers.

Jatinder couldn't help but pause and admire them and in that moment a soldier appeared. Tall, with broad shoulders and a grey German uniform. Jatinder pressed himself against the wall of the corridor. He was panicking, losing his nerve. What could he say to this man? Should he make out he was going to the toilet?

Would he be as kind to Jatinder as Böll had been?

The man was closer now. He must have seen Jatinder.

But there was no shout.

Then – in the half light – Jatinder saw that the man was pulling a trolley behind him. That was why he'd not seen him. He was walking backwards.

Jatinder's heart banged against his ribs as he moved swiftly through to the end of the carriage and out into the open air. He had a plan. There was no time for fear or for doubt. No time to think what could go wrong. He had to act or not act. All around him was the black of the night sky, dotted with a billion stars. And ten fighter planes glowing in the moonlight. He reached out and touched the first plane's wing tip.

His plan was sabotage.

That word sent a chill through him. He had to fight the urge to race back to his compartment. What he was about to do was dangerous, deadly. What had Böll said? He would be shot on the spot. There would be no protection for him. Had Böll really known that this was his plan? Or had he just been making conversation?

Sabotage – this was madness. He'd go back to his compartment. He'd be safe in British hands by the end of the next day. No need to risk his freedom. Or his life.

As he made his decision, Jatinder could see the man with the trolley make his slow way down the corridor. Headed for Jatinder. It was only a matter of time before Jatinder would be caught, and he had to get rid of the matches and the knife before they could incriminate him.

But then Jatinder's foot knocked against a can and he nearly stumbled. He kneeled to see what was in the can. Petrol. The unmistakable smell of petrol.

Jatinder took the matches out of his pocket and stared at them. 'Just throw them off the train,' he told himself. 'Then no one can accuse you of planning to start any fires. Then no one can accuse you of being a man intent on sabotage.'

He pulled back his hand, ready to throw the matches away.

And then he thought of Malik. About what he went through. He thought about the 450 bullets shot at his plane and how he had lived for decades with two of those bullets lodged in his leg. He thought about how he had dared, how he had taken risks and survived.

Jatinder picked up the can of petrol from next to his feet.

He would not turn back. He would at least try to be a hero. He would do this in honour of Malik.

FOURTEEN

Jatinder watched as petrol spread across the fabric of the wing of the first plane.

Next, he opened the box of matches. His hands were trembling and match after match was caught by the wind and sent tumbling into the night.

'Get a grip,' Jatinder told himself. 'Before you lose them all.'

He struck another match off the edge of the box. Not a spark. Nothing. Perhaps this wasn't meant to be.

But he did it again, and the match flared a little, then died, leaving a wisp of smoke.

"Come on," Jatinder said, looking back over his shoulder.

He took out two matches this time and struck them together.

They flared, sending a sharp smell up his nose as he dropped them burning onto the wing of the first Fokker.

His plan had been to light the first plane by the wing, then to move down to the next plane and set fire to that. If he could destroy even half of them this way, he would save many lives, even the lives of the German pilots who were going to fly them.

But the plan didn't work out like that.

The flames took a few seconds to catch on the first Fokker. But when they did, they were blown fast down the wing and into the fuselage. The plane was ablaze in seconds. The burst of heat and light was so intense, so astonishing that Jatinder had to step back into the carriage he had come from.

And then there was a roar. Not the wind, not the train, not a hail of bullets, but the first plane igniting and spraying flames down the length of the train away from Jatinder. He watched, eyes wide with amazement, as the flames from one plane moved to the next, then the next. Soon, the blaze had spread to all ten planes and flames lit up the countryside all around. In the darkness, Jatinder saw farm animals fleeing from the sides of the track.

Now he heard voices shouting. At the same time he felt the sudden judder of the train brakes.

He turned to run away from the voices. But he found that he was caught between the Germans and the flames and he could only back away from the door. He could hear footsteps, heavier now, and the shouting getting louder and louder.

The door swung open.

Jatinder saw Böll's face, staring first at
the burning planes. Then he shielded his eyes
from the heat and light and looked at Jatinder.
There were two emotions to read on his face.

The first was horror. That Jatinder had
destroyed the German planes that Böll so
worshipped.

The second was more like the look he'd had
on his face earlier that day when he'd praised
Jatinder for his daring jump into the haystack.

It was admiration.

But that didn't last.

Three armed soldiers burst through the end
of the carriage and shoved Böll out of the way.
Three guns pointed at Jatinder.

Jatinder raised his hands over his head.

Now what?

The soldiers wanted to know the answer to that question too. Now what? They looked to Böll for a lead, waiting for the order to shoot. Böll was the senior officer and one of the soldiers was actually shouting at him, demanding permission.

And all the time the train was slowing down.

Jatinder was sure he heard a soldier say "sabotage" to Böll. Maybe the words were the same in English and German. In that case Jatinder knew he was in trouble. What had Böll said? That sabotage would get you shot dead. On sight. No exceptions.

Jatinder looked into Böll's dark eyes and Böll shook his head almost in sadness, just as another man burst through the end of the carriage. An older man with ribbons and

91

medals on his chest. An officer still more senior than Böll.

Böll saluted and stepped back.

The three soldiers kept their eyes and guns trained on Jatinder as they waited for the order to fire. This was it. Jatinder knew that Böll wouldn't be able to save him now. He was terrified, and he looked down at the rocky ground beside the railway track. And a thought struck him. Could he do what he had done before?

Should he? Could he? Dare he?

Jump?

FIFTEEN

Jatinder grabbed a rail at the side of the carriage and launched himself off the end of the moving train. Gunshots rang out as he landed on his right foot, then began to tumble, awful pain pressing into his ankle, his head, his back.

A second gunshot. Then two more. Again and again. The heat and light of the burning planes as they flashed by. The clanging and clattering of the huge train wheels on the track. The terror, the noise, the painful brightness of the light – it was all too much.

Then darkness. Darkness and the din of the train as it screeched to a halt ahead of him.

Jatinder tried to stand. His ankle was in agony, but he needed to get away. They would find him. He had seconds to escape.

But he felt dizzy, really dizzy, and sick too. The flashing and burning of the planes was still with him. The stink of the fuel as it spread across the canvas. He screwed up his eyes. The pain in his ankle was killing him.

But he had no time for pain.

Jatinder forced himself to open his eyes, to push his hands against the ground so that he could stand.

It was then that he noticed how soft the ground was beneath him.

In fact, it wasn't rough, stony ground, but smooth clean carpet.

He lifted his head. Everything was different. There was no train track, no stench of burning wood and canvas, no night sky filled with angry shouts. Jatinder was no longer a pilot in a war of one hundred years before. He was in his bedroom, in the house at the old airfield.

Jatinder laughed out loud. Not because he was safe and sound and back at Trenchard House, but because he had jumped. He was thrilled that he had jumped, that he had been brave, faced his fear and taken a risk like no other.

Then a knock at the door snapped him out of his laughter.

"Come in," Jatinder called.

"You OK?" Steve was trying to smile, but his face was tense, concerned.

"Yeah," Jatinder said. "I'm OK."

SIXTEEN

Jatinder, Steve and Esther sat in the back room with the lights on low. In front of them were three mugs of hot chocolate and a view of the old airfield. Mist floated between the house and the trees, and in the distance, the old aircraft hangar was caught in a pool of moonlight. It was two in the morning.

Jatinder had explained what had happened. How he had jumped off a train and ended up on the floor of his room in the middle of the night.

"That was quite a dream," Esther said with a laugh when he had finished.

"He didn't say it was a dream," Steve muttered.

"Steven!" Esther snapped. "You have to stop filling the kids' heads with the idea that there are ghosts of old pilots haunting this place. Look out there. There are no walking dead. Everything Jatinder has told us comes from that book you lent him. Or from the photos he's seen in this house."

Jatinder squinted out at the old airfield. Esther's cross tone and the way she had her arms folded told him this was an old argument between the couple. It was something they didn't agree on, which meant that it was something that had happened before.

Maybe.

Steve was right – no one had asked Jatinder if he thought it had been a dream. Or if it had been real.

"I'm not saying history's not real," Esther went on. "Of course it's real. It's in this place. It's in the book you gave Jatinder to read. But that's as far as it goes. Hundreds of pilots flew from here in both wars. And far too many of them didn't make it back. They were killed, lost in action, shot down from the sky. But that doesn't mean they hang out here trying to lure kids back in time to fight the war all over again."

Steve shrugged. "I still think there's more to this place," he said.

"You would," Esther snapped, her hands gripping the sides of her arms.

Jatinder said nothing. It was best he kept out of this.

They all sipped their hot chocolate, and the silence between them grew.

Steve broke it by turning to Jatinder. "What plane were you flying?" he asked.

"Sopwith Camel," Jatinder replied.

Steve leaned forward. The light caught the side of his face and cast it in shadows. "How do you know?" he asked.

"The plane was just like Malik's."

"Like in the book," Esther interrupted. "That's my point. It's all from the book."

Steve shrugged again. Then he grinned. "Tomorrow," he said, "after training, let's go to the RAF Museum in London. They have a 'First World War in the Air' show on just now. And there's a Sopwith Camel. What do you say?"

"Yeah." Jatinder nodded. "I'd love that."

SEVENTEEN

Out on the pitch the next morning, Jatinder knew exactly what he had to do.

Not think about the night before.

Not think about that afternoon's trip to the RAF Museum.

Just think about football – about playing football to the best of his ability.

It was day three of the summer school. They had done a lot of drills and training, played a few short matches. But today was the first full match. The children were put into two teams. The winning team would get a reward.

"What reward?" Rachel asked.

"A round of applause," the head coach said with a grin.

"Hmmm," Rachel said. "Great."

For Jatinder the first two or three minutes were tricky. His ankle hurt. But he told himself it was only a bit of stiffness. Not a tear, just a strain. If he ran it off it would be OK.

So he ran. And he ran. And he tackled and he passed and – with a minute to go in the game, tied at 2–2 – Rachel earned a free kick.

This time Jatinder pulled her up off the ground.

"Yours," he said, and handed her the ball.

Rachel shook her head. "Yours," she echoed.

Jatinder smiled, nodded and placed the ball on the ground. Then he squinted at the keeper. He saw the keeper squint back at him.

Here he was again. Free kick time. What was he going to do?

Three steps back. He had eyes only for the goal.

He breathed in, breathed out, stepped up and struck the ball for the top right corner. The ball flew hard and true, skimming the top of the bar and going out for a goal kick.

No goal.

Dead ball.

"Good effort," Jatinder heard Greg shout from behind him.

And it was. A good effort. He'd had a go. He was glad about that. Even if he'd missed, what did it matter?

Jatinder gave Greg a thumbs-up and jogged backwards for the goal kick.

EIGHTEEN

"I'm going to check out the First World War show," Jatinder said to Steve, Rachel and Greg as soon as they arrived at the RAF Museum. He couldn't wait, he had to see those planes.

"Great," Steve said. "We'll get a drink first. Come on, you two. See you in a bit, Jatinder."

Jatinder jogged into the First World War building. He passed two planes that weren't Sopwith Camels, and then he found himself in the main hall. There were at least ten planes in the hall among giant screens and glass display cases. He knew right away which one was the Sopwith Camel. It was hanging from the ceiling with its wings tipped, as if it was angling in to attack a target.

Jatinder stopped and stared. He gazed up at the plane from below. From the front, the back, the sides. From every angle.

It was amazing to see the plane without feeling the pressure of being shot at or being about to crash. It had two brown-green wings, one over the other. A short body with a shiny metal nose and a varnished wooden propeller. There were red, white and blue circles painted on the wings and on the body of the plane.

Next, Jatinder ran up a set of white stone stairs to look at the plane from the viewing balcony. His heart thumped and he held onto the railing, almost knocked over by a sudden dizzy feeling

That was when he knew.

He recognised the guns, the shape of the wings, the wires that held the plane together like a kite. And the cockpit with its leather trim around the screen. The four dials. He hadn't read about these details in Malik's book. He only recognised them because he had seen them, been in the midst of them, the plane around him almost a part of him.

It had all happened.

Jatinder was certain of that.

Somehow. Out there, wherever he had been.

And if it had happened, then that meant he had done it all too.

He had jumped out of a plane. Been a prisoner. The enemy had threatened to shoot him for sabotage. He had escaped from a locked train carriage. He had set fire to ten planes. Been shot at. Jumped.

He had done it all.

And he could do more. He could do anything. He could try anything.

He could step up and act. He could take a risk, even if it went wrong. So what if it went wrong? It could go right, too – but only if he took the risk. And Jatinder knew that was the kind of person he wanted to be. He would be a boy who could face death and smile.

ABOUT FLYBOY

The First World War began in 1914 and ended in 1918.

It began with soldiers charging across fields at one another on horses. It ended with hundreds of miles of trenches that faced each other across those same fields, trenches that moved no more than a few yards, year after year. As the war went on, both sides invented more and more powerful bombs to kill more and more of the men in those trenches. Tanks were invented, too, and they only added to the toll of death.

Planes were also used in warfare in the First World War.

The early planes were used to spy on the enemy. Each side used planes to check where their enemy was and what they were doing. But that soon changed.

Each side developed planes to shoot down planes on spy missions. Then they made those planes fly at ever faster speeds and with more powerful guns, so they could attack the enemy in the air. Then planes were fitted with bombs.

Brave young men flew the thousands of planes that were built to perform all these wartime tasks. Hardit Singh Malik was one of those young men. Unlike Jatinder in *Flyboy* and the ghost that haunts him, Malik was a real man.

Malik was desperate to be a pilot. But he was from India and he was banned from flying at first because he wasn't white. The Royal Flying Corps didn't want black or Asian people in their planes. They had old-fashioned racist beliefs and claimed that only white people would be any good as pilots.

They were wrong, of course.

Hardit Singh Malik fought this prejudice to become the first ever Sikh pilot to fly planes of war. When I discovered that he had been shot down and survived and had two bullets in his leg until the day he died, I wanted to know more.

And so I read his book. The same book that Jatinder reads in *Flyboy*.

His book inspired me to make Malik a hero for a modern-day boy – for Jatinder.

Malik lived a long and happy life. After the war, he was a diplomat for India, and his family is very proud of everything he did.

For my research, I read a lot of books about the airmen of the First World War. Two of the things that Jatinder does in *Flyboy* are based on real events I read about in those books.

The first event involved an American airman called Howard Clayton Knotts. Knotts was shot down in 1918 and became a prisoner of war. But when he was on a train to a prisoner-of-war camp he escaped and set fire to seven German bi-planes that were also on the train.

This was a massive risk. Because Knotts was a prisoner of war, the Germans had to look after him. But if he committed sabotage he could be shot by a firing squad, and he would have known that. Knotts was caught after he sabotaged the planes, but he was spared death. His bravery amazed me and I wanted Jatinder to show the same bravery in *Flyboy*.

The other story is about a German pilot called Franz Fritsch. His plane was shot down and burst into flames mid-air. Fritsch climbed out onto the wing of his plane and jumped 300 feet towards a haystack. But, tragically, he missed the haystack and died. When I read about his act of heroism, I wished that he had been successful.

So, *Flyboy* is inspired by three stories from the First World War. One about an Indian, one about an American, one about a German. At the time, the war of 1914 to 1918 was known as the Great War, but as these stories show it was a war that affected people from all over the world, and so it became known as the First World War.

TOM PALMER

ACKNOWLEDGEMENTS

Lots of people have helped me to write this book. I would like to thank them all. My wife and my daughter for their ideas, feedback and support. Also Jim Sells, Phillip Clayton and his excellent colleagues at the two RAF Museums in Cosford and Hendon. The children and teachers of All Saints Primary School in Halifax and Albrighton Primary School next to the Cosford RAF base. The three members of my writing group, James Nash, Anna Turner and Ali Taft. Thanks also to Jatinder Singh and Jagdeep Birdi. Finally, thanks to my agent, David Luxton, and everyone at Barrington Stoke for the passion and intensity of their work.

Our books are tested
for children and young people by
children and young people.

Thanks to everyone who consulted on
a manuscript for their time and effort in
helping us to make our books better
for our readers.